CLAIMING HIS OMEGA

Juno Wells

BLURB

Azaria and Daisy were both kidnapped from their Omega convent and sold at a Klinok auction. The two are separated, sold to different buyers, with Daisy landing in a good situation. Daisy's Alpha, Ryder, helps rescue Azaria, and after Quinn Strang assists Azaria during her forced estrus at his brother's request, they go their separate ways. She doesn't expect to see him again, but when the gangster who originally bought her tracks her to Paladin, she has no choice but to call him for help.

Quinn recruits his brother and

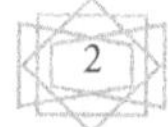

Ryder's friend, Remy, to help rescue the Omega he walked away from weeks ago. He hasn't stopped thinking about her, and once he rescues her from Aldrich Garros, he's going to do what he should have done then—claim her despite all the reasons he didn't the first time.

CHAPTER ONE

Azaria had never felt like this in her life, so hot, itchy, and frantic. Whatever the Klinoks had given her to induce artificial estrus was ravaging her system. Thanks to the low-dose suppressant they used at the convent, she'd never been through such an intense estrus before. She was afraid she was going to die before she could get relief.

She tugged fitfully at her jumpsuit, the one the aliens had given her when they kidnapped her and her friend Daisy from their planet last week. It felt intolerably itchy, and she kept tugging, desperate to have the fabric away from her skin. She wasn't yet far enough gone to strip it off mindlessly though, especially since the Klinok who'd loaded her onto a cart was now trundling her up a ramp to the stage.

She knew Daisy had been sold first, though she had no idea to whom. She'd already been locked in this state of misery and unable to notice—not that she'd had a view of the stage anyway.

She had a view now, and her eyes widened at all the Alphas before her. They were mostly human males, though there were some aliens mixed in as well. She wondered if they were as drawn to human Omega women as the human Alphas were, but it didn't matter. Anyone who could ease this ache would have to do.

She shuddered at the thought, still possessing enough control to be horrified by the idea of mating with someone she barely knew, who had paid for the privilege, and likely wouldn't give a whit about who she was as a person, or what she was like out of estrus.

The emcee reminded the potential buyers she'd been given an enhancer, and a roar went through the crowd. She swore several of them surged forward, requiring the Klinoks acting as the guards between the stage and the buyers to step forward in a unified fashion. That seemed to soothe the fervor of the crowd a little, and the guards stepped back a moment later.

Azaria tried to follow the bidding, wanting to know who was going to end up purchasing her. She had no intention of staying any longer than she had to, but since she was afraid she would instantly capitulate to any Alpha in her current state, she wanted to know what she was getting into before she had a chance to escape.

Unfortunately, the intensity of estrus made it impossible to focus. She was vaguely aware that the bidding abruptly stopped, and a murmur of unease went through the room. She opened her eyes long enough to focus on three Alphas who stepped forward. They were all rough-looking, and two of the three bore facial scars. The third one was the biggest Alphas she'd ever seen, and she shivered.

The biological imperative from being an Omega forced her to admire his size and speculated he would be a good sire, but Azaria squashed that thought. That was still possible with her pheromones being screened, and the box keeping her from smelling any of the Alphas. With three of them bidding on her, she shuddered as she imagined her fate. They were likely combining their funds to buy their own Omega toy. Would they be content with just one cycle of estrus, or would they keep her locked away to pull out each month to use as they saw fit?

It was enough to bring tears to her eyes, and she blinked rapidly before wiping them away with her bare arm. She frowned at the feel of her skin against her face and looked down, shocked she had somehow stripped herself of the itchy jumpsuit. She had no recollection of doing so, and she was appalled that instinct had taken over to that level. Hastily, she grasped the fabric and held it to her front again, but she'd already revealed her nudity to all the buyers.

None of them seemed inclined to counter the bid of the three Alphas though, and she was sold to them in less than a minute. She closed her eyes and leaned back against the clear wall of the box, struggling to calm down and steel herself for what lay ahead.

Azaria lost track of time after that, when her world became nothing but need, pain, and the fever burning through her. She was partially aware of going through an airlock sometime later, and then she found herself in a cargo hold. After that, the big Alpha she'd seen earlier picked up her box seemingly with no effort and carried her from the cargo bay and down corridors.

She lost track again, not becoming aware until a flashing light hurt her eyes. She moaned and put her arm up to cover her face. "What are you doing?" She wanted the question to come out demanding and forceful, but it sounded slurred, like she'd been drinking far too heavily. Having been into Mother Risa's dandelion wine just once in her life, she'd learned not to do that.

"Say hello to the boss," said the big Alpha. His cohorts chuckled.

She was confused. "What? Who's there?"

"Leave us," said a voice. It sounded deep and rough, with a forceful edge that made her tremble. Part of it was her Omega responding to the authority of the Alpha's tone, but part of it was just blatant fear.

She heard the hydraulic hiss of the door opening a moment later, and then it closed again. She expected someone to step into sight, but all she heard was that voice once more.

"They did a fine job. I would've

preferred they pick up both Omegas that were for sale, but the fools were running late, and it had already been done. They did send a couple of people after the purchaser, but since they never showed up, I assume that prize is lost." He sounded mournful.

Azaria realized he must be talking about Daisy, but she couldn't bring herself to care about the fate of the Alpha who had bought her friend. If he'd been killed by two others, the only reason she cared was because it meant there were twice as many for Daisy to deal with. Since her friend was less confident and on the sweeter side, she wasn't sure how Daisy could cope with such a thing.

"You're still a fine treasure indeed, Omega."

The way he purred that word made her shiver in pleasure as much she hated the reaction. What she wouldn't give to be free of this biological imperative to respond to an Alpha when she was in this state. She tried to make herself glare as she looked around. "Where are you?"

"I'm at home, Omega. You're *en route* there now, and we'll be united within a few hours."

She couldn't help moaning at the thought, but it wasn't from desire. It was pure agony at the idea of enduring this torture for hours longer. "Hurts now. Make it stop."

He laughed, seeming unbothered by her pain. "The only way I could do that would be to allow the Alphas on my crew to have a go at you. That might happen in the future, but I insist on the first taste."

As he started to speak to her, vile words spewing from his mouth while he described in great detail what he planned to do to her, Azaria allowed the haze of fever to slip over her. She didn't want to hear his words. There was nothing seductive about them, and they turned her stomach. She had no idea who he was or what he looked like, but she was already repulsed by him.

Only the Omega inside her was clamoring for the Alpha in him, but it was because he was an Alpha, not because of whoever the Alpha was. It was all biology and instinct, and she was disgusted by her inability to control it, though it was wired into her very nature.

Before completely losing track of her surroundings and awareness of what was happening, Azaria assured herself she would do her best to fight the man who'd bought her. He might be an Alpha, and she might be forced to temporarily submit due to biology, but it didn't sound like he planned to claim her.

He wouldn't if he were going to share her with his men at some point in the future, and that gave her a chance to escape. She wouldn't have the protection of an Alpha's claim and his scent infusing hers, but she also wouldn't have the burden of being bonded to a man she hated, and she was already certain she would hate the Alpha who felt entitled to buy her.

Azaria's eyes opened sometime later, though she had no idea how long it had been. She thought she was still in the same room, but something was different. She forced her eyes open wider, blinking back the sweat that dripped from her forehead. She was burning up, and she'd once again discarded the jumpsuit. It laid on the floor beside her, but she didn't bother to reach for it. She felt too weak and shaky, and then she was distracted by the sight of a large Alpha bending down in front of the box.

He wasn't quite as big as the one who'd carried her in, but he was close. With his long, white-blond hair, scruffy stubble, and huge muscles, he looked like a savage barbarian. He was most certainly an Alpha, and she whimpered in need. "Make it stop hurting, Alpha."

If he heard her words, he didn't respond for a moment. He did press his palm to the box, and she did the same as she said again, "Alpha." Her word emerged more comprehensible this time.

"Omega," said the man with a hint of reluctance. There was tender concern in his voice, but there was just as much hesitation, and even in her current state, she realized the Alpha didn't want to be here.

She couldn't care about that now. She was hurting so much that she just needed relief. She whimpered as she looked past him, eyes widening at the sight of Daisy before her. She mouthed her friend's name, but she was unable to speak.

After a moment, Daisy turned to the man beside her, and Azaria had never seen him before. Due to the resemblance between him and the Alpha standing near her box, she assumed they were related, but she had no idea how they had come to be here, or why Daisy was here either. For a moment, she feared the man who'd bought her had found a way to steal Daisy away from the Alpha who'd purchased her as well.

It hurt too much to try to focus,

and she was unaware again until her box shifted, pressing her against one wall. She opened her eyes and realized she was being carried on her side by the Alpha who was holding the box on his shoulder as though she and it weighed nothing.

He was saying something to Daisy, who stood in front of him in a challenging way, but her view didn't allow her to get even a glimpse of Daisy's lips to guess what her friend was saying, and she was too incoherent with fever from estrus to understand what they were saying. After a moment, Daisy stepped aside, and the Alpha carrying her marched past.

She fuzzed out again, once more losing awareness until her box was turned upright, and she slumped to the floor of it. She opened her eyes in time to see Daisy and the other man stepping onto a skid, and she realized she was on a different one with the Alpha who'd carried her. She whimpered, a hint of fear at the sight of Daisy departing, but mostly from pain and need.

The skid ride to his ship seemed to take forever, and she was surprised to be aware enough to read the name on the side as they approached the cargo hold. *Catriona*. It was a lovely name, and she wondered how his ship had acquired such a moniker. He seemed like the rough and brutal type, more prone to have a ship named something like *Starkiller* than a woman's name.

The thought left her when the skid entered his cargo bay, and he picked up the box to carry her through his freighter moments later. He took her to his bedroom. She recognized that enough even in her current state to know his intentions. She was all for them at the moment, held in the grip of artificial estrus and hurting from it.

When he didn't open the box, she scratched at it with her nails and whimpered at him.

"In a moment, Azaria. We need to talk first."

She moaned and shook her head, rejecting the idea. She didn't need talk. She needed him to ease this ache inside her.

"My name is Quinn, and I want to help you."

She put her palm to the clear box again. "Alpha." She couldn't hide the need and pain in her tone.

He flinched as though she'd struck him. "It has to be your choice, Azaria. I promised Daisy that, and I would've anyway. I don't have any suppressant, but I have sedative. I can knock you out for a while until I can get you some suppressant if that's what you want."

She shook her head. "I want you, Alpha. Make it stop hurting."

He closed his eyes, clearly struggling. "I'm offering you an alternative, one that you won't regret later. I can get the sedative right now."

"Please, it hurts." She pounded against the box as she cried the words.

After another long second, his shoulders slumped, and he nodded. "Very well. Try to remember I gave you a different choice."

With those words, he moved

closer to the box, pressing a hand to the top of it, and the entire thing opened seconds later, the walls collapsing to the floor.

Azaria jumped up even as he reached down to help her, pressing her body against his and pulling frantically at his flight suit and armor. She wanted him inside her more than anything she'd ever wanted in her entire life, and she was beyond rational thought. "Take me."

"Fuck," he said, sounding defeated before his mouth claimed hers in a long, intense kiss.

It curled her toes and sent heat spiraling through her, but it wasn't enough. It wasn't nearly enough to ease the agony inside her, and she continued to tug ineffectually at his clothing, wanting to strip him.

"Hold on." He broke the kiss, gently pushing her back. Azaria refused to be denied, and she rushed forward again, clawing at his clothes.

"Stop," he said in a tone full of authority.

She froze under the impact of it, unable to deny the effect it had on her. She trembled, but she didn't move forward. She whimpered, begging for mercy.

"I'm just getting undressed." He did so quickly, with an economical grace of movement that she found compelling even in her current haze.

When he was as nude as her, she rushed forward again, able to break the command he'd placed through sheer need and desire. She launched herself at him, and he lifted and carried her to the bed. He laid her down with her face on the pillow, and she grasped it as he lifted her hips. His shaft was large, and she braced herself for both the pleasure and pain of it entering her. She was producing copious amounts of slick, and it eased his way, but she'd never taken a lover before, and it hurt unbearably for a moment, enough to cut through the pain and drive of estrus to make her howl with anguish.

"Fuck," he said again. "Hold still, Azaria. Breathe through it."

His words were hard to understand in her current state, but the soothing tone helped her relax. She was able to surrender and lose herself again, blunting her awareness as he drove into her over and over.

She was thrusting back against him just as eagerly, needing to feel joined with him. She cried out as she started to come, burying her face in the pillow and biting it with her teeth to stifle the sound as her sheath contracted around him. He continued to pump in and out of her, moving more forcefully now, and though her flesh was sensitive, she didn't shy away from his rough possession. She felt herself coming again within minutes, and this time, his shaft twitched inside her as he found release too.

She grunted at the feel of his fluid splashing her insides. She'd never experienced anything like it, and she wanted more. Her sheath automatically tightened around him, milking him of every drop, and then his knot formed, locking them together.

She slumped forward against the pillow, temporarily sated. As estrus faded and awareness returned, she remembered she was joined with a man she didn't know. She wasn't certain how she'd arrived on the ship, and now she wondered if she'd imagined Daisy's presence? Had she been hallucinating in the thralls of estrus? The fever burned hotly enough that it was a possible side effect for a woman trapped in it too long without relief, at least according to the biology classes she'd taken at the convent during her education.

He didn't speak, so she found it difficult to as well. They were joined in an awkward way, but at least she wasn't forced to look at him, to meet his gaze and see the knowledge of what they'd done reflected back at her.

Perhaps it was a courtesy he'd extended taking her this way, face down and from behind, but it felt demeaning, and she was chafing to escape. As soon as he started to soften, she scrambled forward, disengaging before it was strictly comfortable for either one of them, but ignoring the twinge of discomfort.

She hastily rolled over, grabbing the blanket from the bed and wrapping it around her as she turned to face him. "Who are you, and why am I here?"

If he found her question strange, he showed no sign of it.

He also didn't appear to be ready to answer as he turned away from her. She thought he was going to walk away, but all he did was move to the dresser to retrieve a new flight suit from a drawer. He donned it before turning back to face her, and she felt better when they were both clothed—though her clothing consisted of a blanket for the moment.

"My name is Quinn Strang, and you're here because Daisy and Ryder asked me to help rescue you."

She scowled. "How the heck would Daisy know you? She's never left Paladin."

He shrugged a shoulder. "I

gather her acquaintance with Ryder is recent, but he's my brother. He asked me to help you after explaining what kind of state you'd be in."

She let out a shaky breath as her face flooded with heat. This was different from the raging fire of fever. It was strictly from humiliation at what she'd been reduced to, and how she had acted with a man she didn't know. She looked away from him. "I'd like to go back to the convent."

She expected no objection. After all, he seemed to have no interest in claiming her. He hadn't even nuzzled her scent glands or made any effort to do anything besides relieve her as efficiently as possible. She told herself that was a good thing, because she didn't want to be bound to an Alpha she didn't know, and particularly one who seemed apathetic about her existence.

"That's fine. You can use the comm system to call Ryder and ask him to take you. I have a salvage operation I have to get back to."

Tears burned her eyes for a moment, and she blinked them back hastily before nodding. She was careful not to look at him, not wanting him to see the betraying moisture in her eyes. Part of Azaria had assumed she would never even find an Alpha, since she'd planned to stay on Paladin at the convent for the rest of her life.

As a younger girl, when she'd occasionally indulged in fantasies of perhaps finding her ideal Alpha—not that she bought into that silly fairytale—it had always been a romantic experience, clouded by vagueness in her mind, and leaving her feeling loved and protected. It certainly hadn't left her feeling used and discarded like this, and the reality was so much worse than her fantasies.

Of course, it could have been even worse. She could've ended up in the possession of the man who'd tried to buy her and sent his crew to retrieve her. Eventually, he would've passed her on to them, and that would've been far harsher.

She started walking away from him, holding the blanket carefully around herself when he called her name. She froze and looked back at him. "Yes…Quinn?" It took her a moment to remember his name, which shamed her and seemed to irk him. She should at least know that about him before breeding with him.

"You don't have to worry about getting pregnant," he said gruffly.

Her eyes widened, since she hadn't yet considered the

possibility. "How do you know? It's the only time I'm fertile, and you're an Alpha, so…?" She trailed off with a shrug, having every intention of acquiring a preventative as soon as possible.

He shook his head. "It's impossible. I had a vasectomy years ago."

"Oh." She exhaled in relief, denying the small surge of unhappiness at the idea of not creating life. That was strictly the biological imperative of the Omega reacting, and not her own rational brain.

She certainly didn't want to be a single mother left to raise a child with an Alpha who couldn't be trusted. Or raise it alone. Her mother had ended up in that position, and if she hadn't found Paladin and Mother Risa before Azaria's birth, Azaria might've had a similar fate. She was grateful to be spared that much, at least.

Without another word to him, she quickly donned her jumpsuit before exiting his room and making her way to a comm station nearby. He followed behind, programming the frequency for her before walking past. He disappeared around the corridor, and the other blond man she vaguely remembered seeing from before appeared on the screen.

She talked with him for a moment, arranging transport to his ship, and then made her way to the cargo bay. She helped herself to Quinn's spare E-suit and stepped into the airlock, waiting until the pincer arm from the *Remedy* appeared moments later before grasping it and allowing it to tow her inside the ship housing her friend and the man who'd somehow come into Daisy's life.

She suspected he'd purchased her, and she was determined to hate him for that. If possible, she would do herself and Daisy the biggest favor ever by disposing of the Alpha. They could take his ship and return to Paladin, where they belonged.

CHAPTER TWO

Quinn was trying not to think about Azaria, and how neatly she'd fit together with him, how her sheath had conformed to accommodate his size, and how good it had felt to drive into an Omega again, even though she wasn't his bonded mate.

He let out a sigh of disgust with himself as the comm system buzzed once more. He was surprised to see Ryder appear, since his brother and his ship had departed at least half an hour ago.

"Do you need something? Did you change your mind about borrowing money?"

He'd been lucky enough to have a few decent salvages recently, and he knew Ryder hadn't been so lucky. He'd spent most of what he'd earned smuggling rathium to liberate Daisy, but he was unsurprised when his brother shook his head.

"I told you, I'll work it out. I was just making sure this is what you really want, Quinn. It's the last chance before we enter ionospace. You seem kind of lost."

Quinn snorted. "I've been lost for four years, seven months, three days, and…" He glanced at the timekeeper on the screen, "Eighteen minutes."

His brother flinched and then nodded. "I just wanted to make sure you didn't want to keep her."

Quinn snorted. "We don't all live in a fairytale, brother. Just because you happened to luck out and find your ideal Omega by purchasing her at an auction doesn't mean it's going to work out that way for the rest of us. Azaria seems like a fine woman, and maybe she'll be happy someday with a different Alpha, but it won't be me. I don't want another Omega ever again."

He spoke firmly, though there was just the faintest trace of regret in his words. He sincerely meant them, but he wished he were capable of not meaning them. He wished he could embrace another opportunity, but it was easy enough to recall what had happened last time that it helped him quell the urge. "Take care of her, Spud."

With a groan at the nickname, Ryder nodded, and then he was gone.

Quinn realized he was still sitting in the same place he'd been since they hijacked Garros's ship. That was a dangerous spot to be, because the gangster would soon realize his ship and crew had never shown up. Already, there could be more of his people *en route* to investigate and rescue those aboard the *Stargazer*. Of course, from Garros's reputation, he was far more likely to kill the survivors for failing than he was to save them, so he'd have no hesitation killing Quinn as well.

He abruptly programmed a destination, uncaring if it was his final one. He just wanted to get away from the area, so he entered ionospace seconds later. The computer revealed he was on course for the wreckage of ships near the asteroid belt where he'd been successfully scavenging for a while now.

There was a lot of competition

around that area, but there were plenty of wrecks so far. He had planned to strip a few more before moving to a different location when Ryder's call came in. It was as good a place as any to return and finish his work.

As he flew, he tried not to let his thoughts wander to Azaria. Her long, lean body was appealing to him, and he wished he'd taken time to feel the weight of her breast in his hands rather than just quickly copulate to ease her pain and be done.

He'd made it as unemotional as possible, fervently wanting to avoid any entanglements between the two of them. He didn't want an Omega falling for him, and he was certainly in no spot to feel protective and loving toward one again.

After the way it had ended with Catriona, he grimaced at the thought. Azaria's sleek black hair, dark-brown eyes, and coppery-brown skin would remain with him, but no emotion could be allowed to hang around. He could pull out images of her when he needed inspiration while he was pleasuring himself, but he absolutely refused to feel anything for the delicate Omega. He'd been there once before, and he would never make that mistake again.

Yet she lingered in his mind

long after he allowed her to actively do so, and no matter how many times he tried to push her out of his memory, he was still vaguely aware of an ache from her lack of presence. Thank goodness he'd only bred her once, because she was dangerous. An Omega like Azaria could cause him to forget his resolve and end up falling in love all over again. He refused to do that, so he was happy he would never see her again.

Really, he was.

CHAPTER THREE

Azaria had been back at Paladin for three days now, and Daisy had already been gone again for two of them. She missed her friend, but the restlessness inside was from more than just having Daisy go off with her Alpha.

She worried for her friend, though she was convinced by now Ryder was the atypical Alpha, one who actually cared about protecting his Omega and others weaker than him. He didn't seem like the kind of Alpha who took advantage of his superior strength and legal standing to do whatever he wanted to an Omega, as long as he didn't kill her. From what she'd learned at the convent, that was a truly rare Alpha indeed.

She still was uncertain if Quinn was of the same cut, but she doubted it. He'd seemed to be providing perfunctory help at the least amount possible, and she should be grateful he'd kept it all physical and not tried to introduce anything more emotional between them. She shouldn't be missing him with a constant dull ache in her chest, and she shouldn't be feeling like she was suddenly out of place in the place that had been her home all her life.

She'd been born on Paladin, right in the walls of the convent, and before the Klinoks had kidnapped her and Daisy, she'd only ever been to a nearby moon to trade with the Beta farmers there. Everything should have been familiar and easy, but it suddenly felt too small and constricting.

Nothing was like it had been. Nothing felt like it fit her anymore. The daily contemplation, the quiet moments, and even the chores didn't distract her from her morose thoughts and feeling something was missing. Out of desperation, thinking perhaps the estrus had brought her to this state, and the drug used to induce it had done something to damage her, she approached Mother Risa on the fourth morning after her return home.

Risa was in the garden, plucking weeds alongside other sisters. Her hands were covered with dirt, and she seemed right at home there. Azaria envied her that as she knelt beside the Mother Superior and started to help weed.

"It's good to see you getting back into the routine," said Risa.

Azaria drew in a sharp breath and exhaled, looking around for a moment to make sure the nearest sister wasn't close enough to hear her before she turned her head fully to Mother Risa. "I don't feel like I am. Something's different. I'm completely out of sorts. May I talk with you?"

"Of course." Risa looked down at the weeds for a moment and then looked up at her. "I suppose these can wait." She got to her feet with gracefulness and wiped her hands before gesturing for Azaria to precede her.

Azaria just brushed her hands down her robe, since she'd barely touched dirt, and made her way to Mother Superior's office. When she was inside, Risa followed right behind her and closed the door. She was unable to suppress the urge to pace back and forth.

Risa just watched her quietly for a moment before stepping forward and putting a hand on her shoulder. "Try to relax and tell me what's bothering you."

Azaria let out a small sigh. "I think that enhancer they gave me did something to me. I feel different, and not in a good way. I'm unsettled. I'd like to request a higher dose of suppressant."

Risa frowned. "We have you on the best dose to still maintain a natural cycle."

"I don't want to feel like this anymore," said Azaria with anger before bursting into tears. She turned away from Risa to bury her face in her hands, taking a moment to compose herself before turning back to the other woman. "It has to be the hormones or something. Please, Mother Risa, I'm begging you."

After a moment, Risa sighed. "I don't agree with completely suppressing all parts of the Omega, but it isn't my decision to make. I want you to go see Sister Kathleen. As long as you're medically sound, I'll authorize the maximum dose of suppressants, but I don't think it's the problem."

"It has to be," said Azaria

firmly. She refused to entertain the idea of it being anything else. With a nod toward the Mother Superior, she left her office and rushed down the hall to the medical wing.

Sister Kathleen ushered her inside the room with a smile and nodded to the table. "Take a seat and tell me what's wrong."

Azaria quickly explained her purpose for being there, not missing the disapproval in Sister Kathleen's expression when she turned back to her. "No one knows the long-term effects of using that much suppressant. It could be detrimental to your health in the long run. It will most certainly blunt all your normal responses, so I don't advise this."

She firmed her shoulders. "I understand the risks, but I intend to take them."

With a sigh, but no further protestation, Sister Kathleen examined her for the next few minutes. When she finished, she looked up at Azaria. Her expression was impossible to read, but she seemed troubled by something. "I must speak with Mother Risa, and then she'll be in to see you."

Azaria grimaced as the sister left, suspecting she was on her way to try to dissuade Risa from agreeing to allow her to increase her suppressants. She hoped the sister wasn't successful in doing so as she clenched her hands on her lap, counting the minutes that seemed to drag by forever before Mother Risa entered the exam room sometime later.

"I'm afraid you can't increase your suppressants, Azaria."

She frowned. "I understand Kathleen has reservations, as do you, but it's my choice—"

"I would agree it's your choice, but there's no reason to do so. It could even be dangerous in your current state."

Azaria's stomach clenched with dread. "What current state?"

"Sister Kathleen tells me you're newly pregnant."

Her mouth dropped open with shock, and she shook her head instinctively. "I can't be. Quinn told me he had a vasectomy."

Risa sniffed. "It's hardly above an Alpha to lie, is it? If he wished for you to carry his seed, he would want to keep you from taking anything to prevent it. It's too late to stop the pregnancy from occurring now, though you can end its progression if you choose."

Azaria froze, the weight of the decision pressing upon her for seconds before she discarded the option. "I don't think I could do that, Mother Risa."

"That is your choice as well. In that case, you know you're still most welcome here at the convent. My own mother gave birth to me here, as did yours."

Azaria nodded. "I appreciate that." She recalled how closed the convent had become to Daisy once her friend accepted Ryder as her Alpha. She was thankful to still have the option to remain at her home, and she was hopeful that her feeling out of sorts was attributable to changes in hormones. Surely, she would soon be back to normal?

"Of course, if you involve the Alpha in this, you'll have to leave the planet." Mother Risa didn't seem completely unsympathetic. "It's a difficult choice."

Azaria nodded, though she already felt like she'd made it. If he had truly tricked her into believing she couldn't get pregnant so she would be forced to, he wasn't likely the kind of influence she'd want to expose her child to, though she couldn't deny there was a niggle of guilt at the idea of not telling him.

She spent the next few days in quiet contemplation while focusing on trying to fit back in with life at the convent. Had it always been this restrictive? She knew it had, but until she'd experienced the bigger world, it had seemed completely normal and just fine.

She was the one who'd changed, not the environment around her, and she was desperate to change back. Was such a thing feasible though? She wondered if that were possible for anyone. Change was clearly possible, but was it plausible to assume one could devolve to a previous state?

Yet how could she leave this planet? The only safe way to do so was with an Alpha who claimed her and protected her with his scent. She was doubtful any Alpha would want her since she was pregnant with another Alpha's child. Perhaps once the baby was born, she would be able to attract an Alpha if she chose, but would he accept her child?

It seemed the only option available was Quinn, but she refused to consider the idea. One afternoon, as she seriously contemplated how she wanted the rest of her life to be, and how she wanted to raise her child, she went so far as to look up Quinn's comm frequency and program it into her wrist comm, but she couldn't bring herself to press the button to connect the communication. Instead, she pushed aside making the decision once more and tried to immerse herself in the afternoon work detail.

In some ways, Azaria thought she had made progress in becoming more content with staying on Paladin as the weeks progressed. She certainly saw the advantage to raising a child in such a calm environment, and once Sister Kathleen had revealed she was expecting a girl child, she was fearful it too would be an Omega.

Her daughter would be safest raised in an atmosphere like this, though it was a small world confined by many rules. She had mostly resigned herself to the idea, and she hadn't given any serious thought to calling Quinn for at least two weeks, but that changed the morning klaxon alarms rang throughout the convent as something attacked their defense system above the planet.

"To the shelter," said Mother Risa, her voice carrying over the intercom. "Whatever's up there has completely destroyed our security system."

Azaria dropped what she was doing and rushed to join the others heading toward the shelter. She'd had defense training, but it sounded like the weapons they had on the planet were going to be no match for whatever ship or ships had torn through their security system.

It left her doubting if the shelter would be secure either, or at least secure enough to keep out whatever outside force was invading. She trembled at the thought as she put a hand over her tummy, which was just now starting to have a noticeable-to-her bulge. A tremble of fear shot through her, and she vowed to do whatever necessary to protect her child.

Moments later, she was crowded into the shelter with most of the other sisters, noticing Mother Risa had not appeared. She was fearful, and that grew from anxiety to terror when the communication panel on the wall nearby lit up under its own power, meaning someone else had control of the A.I. that ran the convent.

She let out a sharp gasp along with many others at the sight of Mother Risa being held in an Alpha's arms, his gun pressed to her forehead.

"Today, we've only come for one of you. Surrender yourself peacefully, and the rest of you will be left alone… For now." His dark chuckle didn't inspire confidence.

There was whispering around her as they speculated who might be the target. Azaria's heart squeezed with fear, and she was unsurprised when the man said, "Surrender yourself, Azaria Khalid."

She'd known from the moment she saw him he must be from the same group of men who had bought her at the auction and planned to take her to Aldrich Garros. She didn't think she'd seen him before, but he wore the same all-black outfit as the others, and more than that, there was an air of menace about him that had hovered over all of them, even the Beta males she'd seen while being transported onto the ship.

Silence reigned inside the shelter, and gazes moved to her,

some with sympathy, while others bore clear disapproval or outright anger. There were more of the latter than the former.

There was no choice to be made. She knew if she didn't walk voluntarily from the shelter, it was likely some of the sisters around her would make the decision for her. If they had to choose between trying to survive the attack and losing Mother Risa, or surrendering one of the sisters from the convent, they had an obvious choice before them.

She could hardly blame them for that, though her heart was sticking in her throat when she moved to the exit and pressed the button. The door opened with a hydraulic hiss, and as soon as she passed through, it closed again. She heard someone lock it behind her, and she trembled as she walked up the stairs to reach the ground level.

When she stepped out of the shelter, she found three Alphas waiting for her, all holding guns. They were hardly likely to need them against one unarmed Omega, but she didn't point that out. She didn't speak to them at all or even look at them as she walked forward, intent on reaching the man who held Mother Risa. She stopped a few feet from him. "Release her."

He looked at one of the men standing near her. "Is it her?"

Azaria didn't move as he scanned her before nodding confirmation. At that point, she stretched slightly, pretending she was just shifting position as she pulled up the contact list in her wrist comm.

It took a few more subtle movements spaced over the next five minutes as the men released Mother Risa and marched Azaria toward the ship for her to pull up Quinn's frequency. She hoped he wouldn't answer and betray the call, so she was quick to launch into speaking as soon as she was sure it was about to connect.

"What do you want with me?"

"We don't want anything with you," said the Alpha who'd held Mother Risa prisoner. "Our boss is a different matter."

"Who's your boss?" She already knew though.

"Aldrich Garros, and I wouldn't want to be you." He chuckled harder than he had when he'd issued the veiled threat to the other sisters in the shelter. "There's no telling what Garros has planned for a tasty little Omega like you. Once he's tired of you, he'll pass you on like he always does, and then we get a taste too."

She shivered under the threat,

doing her best not to reveal her horror at the idea. She tried to maintain her icy façade. "How long until we reach his planet?"

"Less than a day if we use a boost gate. We have orders to get you back as quickly as possible. Mr. Garros hasn't liked being kept waiting for you, so you're likely going to pay for that too." He seemed unbothered by the notion.

She scoffed at him. "Did he expect me to shun the ability to escape such a fate?"

"I can't speak for his expectations, but I imagine they include you staying where he puts you. You'll do better if you submit right from the start." His voice lowered an octave, taking on a sinister note that was woven through with clear delight. "You can hardly help to do that though, can you, Omega?" He spoke in a deliberately authoritative fashion.

Azaria braced herself for the typical response, but she felt nothing. She had no urge to tremble or submit to him, and she hoped it would be the same with Garros. Could it be the pregnancy was shielding her from the natural biological imperative of an Omega to respond to an Alpha?

It was something to be thankful for, even though she was terrified for the fate of her child and the pregnancy. If it interfered with what Garros wanted from her, she doubted he would balk at ordering someone to remove the child from her body. She'd die trying to stop it, but it wouldn't do anything to save either one of them.

He marched her onto the ship, pausing in the cargo bay to take her wrist comm and anything he must've deemed capable of being turned into a weapon. "Take her to the empty quarters, and make sure you lock her in. I don't want to be like the last crew and lose my head if we lose her."

"Yes, Theos," said the Alpha nearest her. He put his hand on her elbow, holding her tighter than necessary, as he indicated for her to move forward. He was practically moving her at a frog march, and she did her best to keep up with the pace he set, refusing to allow any show of weakness to these Alphas. She hoped she could maintain her resolve and strength in the face of Aldrich Garros as well, though she feared she might yet yield to a man like him.

It wasn't because he was an Alpha that she was terrified. It was because of his reputation, and what she'd learned of him during her brief period of captivity. She also feared him because of the words he'd spoken to her before they ever met, detailing the filthy, awful things he planned to do to her.

Her only hope was Quinn had gotten the communication and would intercept the ship before they reached Garros's planet. If not, there was no hope remaining. The idea of her being able to overpower an Alpha and his minions to escape was laughable. It didn't mean she planned to submit without a fight, but she was realistic enough to know how it was likely to turn out if Quinn didn't come for her.

CHAPTER FOUR

Quinn leaned back in his chair, reeling from what he'd overheard before the one identified as Theos had taken her wrist comm, tossing it aside. From the conversation, they'd been at the convent and were heading back to Garros's planet. He wasn't certain how the mobster had found Azaria, but that he had bothered to look for her was worrisome. It indicated she meant something to him, though it didn't necessarily mean a sentimental value. He might've simply been enraged that she had slipped away, and he was set to remedy that.

Quinn refused to allow such a thing. She might not be his Omega, but when he dreamed of her at night, waking with her name on his lips and sweat coating his body from the dreams he'd had—some pleasing, but most ending with her being torn away from him—it was difficult to remind himself she wasn't. He felt possessive and protective of her, and he refused to allow her to fall into Garros's hands.

Resolved to fix the situation as quickly as possible, he had the computer locate Ryder's position, and he was relieved to see he wasn't too far away. He called his brother with the communication system, and Ryder's face appeared on the screen a moment later.

He looked a lot like Quinn but with short hair and a less hardened demeanor. In particular, Ryder looked almost insanely happy compared to how Quinn felt, and he smothered the dart of envy. He knew that kind of happiness, but he also knew how much it hurt when it ended.

He shoved aside all thoughts of emotion. "I need your help, Ryder."

Ryder's eyes widened, but he didn't hesitate. "Of course. What can I do?"

"I think Azaria Khalid's fallen back into the hands of Garros. I need your help rescuing her, but I'm not sure we can reach the ship before it lands on the planet."

Ryder blanched. "You think we might have to go to Garros's planet itself?"

Quinn nodded, not downplaying the risk. "I know it's a lot to ask, especially from a mated Alpha with an Omega to protect."

"Daisy's expecting too," said Ryder. He looked sick for a moment.

Quinn said, "I understand if you say no."

Ryder's shoulders stiffened. "I'm not going to do that. You helped me when I needed it, as you always have. It's a rare enough occurrence when my older brother comes to me for help, and I'm certainly not going to turn you away. I'll make sure Daisy's tucked away somewhere safe, and I might be able to recruit someone else to help us, but I can't promise that. He has his own Omega and child to look after."

"Any help would be appreciated." After setting up the rendezvous coordinates with his brother, Quinn rang off and turned to stare at the expanse of space around him, though he wasn't seeing the twinkling stars. His thoughts were on Azaria, and what she might be enduring.

At least she was safe for the moment, since it was unlikely Garros had gone on such a menial mission himself to claim her. If they could find her before they reached the planet, he didn't think they'd have much trouble rescuing her. At least if they were going against a ship like the *Stargazer* and had the element of surprise they had last time.

If she reached the planet, that was a different prospect, and he was less hopeful they would succeed. Still, he had to try. She wasn't his Omega, but he wanted to protect and look after her, and he couldn't allow her to remain a prisoner of someone like Garros, who would probably claim her, use her, and discard her when he grew bored.

He met up with his brother almost a day later, and there was another ship accompanying the *Remedy*. This one was identified as *Eve's Sacrifice*, and the captain of it quickly appeared on the screen so Ryder could introduce them.

"Quinn, this is Remy Cruz. He's agreed to help us. I met him a while back, and we happened to be in the same quadrant, so maybe we stand a chance at this."

"Maybe, but I think the ship's already set down on Garros's planet. It disappeared from my ability to track it almost an hour ago." It had probably landed on the planet and was hidden behind planetary shields similar to what the convent planet used.

"We're still doing this," said a voice behind Remy, who turned enough in the direction of the speaker for Quinn to get a glimpse of the woman behind him. It was impossible to tell just by looking at her, but she was likely an Omega.

She held a small child on her hip, and he grimaced. "Perhaps it would be better if you don't join us, Mr. Cruz."

"I think I'll be in bigger trouble with my wife if I don't," said Remy with a crooked smile. His expression changed to one far more serious. "Besides, it sounds like this girl needs help, and that's our imperative, isn't it?"

Quinn shifted uneasily in his seat, not responding. That was his biological imperative, and once upon a time, he'd been a slave to it. He'd protected those who were weaker than him, and he'd foolishly claimed an Omega of his own. He'd never make that mistake again though, but he wondered briefly if he were doing the wrong thing in general, and if

Catriona would disapprove of the actions he'd taken in the intervening years.

That line of thought was too uncomfortable to bear scrutiny, and he shoved it firmly aside. "I suggest we leave the Omegas behind somewhere safe though." He lumped the unknown woman behind Remy into that category, making certain assumptions.

"That won't be necessary," said the woman as she came to stand beside Remy. "We're confident we can help, and it poses no undue risk to our family. If the worst happens, the baby and I will take an escape pod. We have a list of rendezvous points worked out, and Daisy will come with us."

"Daisy's already on Remy and Maya's ship," said Ryder, though he seemed pained to share the information, likely keenly feeling the separation from his Omega. "We thought it was prudent to have both the women together in case they needed to flee. Remy has an S-class life pod, and they'll both be safe. All three," he hastily amended.

"Four," said Daisy, though she didn't appear on the screen with Remy and his Omega.

"Maya is capable of taking care of herself," said Remy with quiet confidence. "She knows what she wants to do, and I support her decision."

He was hardly likely to keep pushing to protect someone else's Omega, so he shrugged a shoulder. "If that's your wish, I accept it. I think we need to discuss how we're going to get onto the planet."

"We have that covered as well."

He turned his attention to the monitor showing his brother. "Oh?"

"Remy has a stealth shield on his ship. It's big enough to encompass all three ships if we fly in tight formation."

Quinn suppressed a surge of envy at the thought. Clearly, Remy and his Omega were doing well for themselves if they could afford that kind of technology, along with the best life pod available, which was impervious to most weapons and had its own built-in A.I., a long-term survival option that included aquaponics, and weapons.

"In that case, send me the coordinates of how to align."

His ship received them a few moments later, and he turned it over to the A.I. to plot the course. Since they had to maintain exact coordinates, and he was a little distracted, he decided manual piloting wasn't the best option at the moment.

Unfortunately, that left him

time to think, and various scenarios came to him, all culminating in the death of the rescue party and leaving Azaria in Garros's hands. He refused to accept that outcome, so he did his best to banish the thoughts from his mind and focus on the mission ahead.

The three ships set down on the planet almost a half-hour later, having to navigate through the security system. It didn't recognize them as a threat, but it still had components that had to be carefully dismantled or bypassed without alerting the planet below they were under attack.

Thanks to Garros's lavishness, it

was easy enough to figure out where to land. There was only one large structure on the planet, and it proved to be an obscenely enormous mansion bracketed by smaller buildings that probably held a variety of supplies and vehicles for both off- and on-planet travel.

Once the ship had landed, Quinn stopped by his armory and gathered as many weapons as he could safely carry while still allowing good range of movement and keeping his hands free. He joined the rest of them moments later, slightly surprised to see just the two men. "I half-expected your Omegas to convince you to let them come along."

"There's no *letting* involved when it comes to Maya," said Remy with a grin. "However, she knows someone besides Swish has to stay with Neve, and I trust her to defend our daughter with her life. It won't come to that though, because we're going to keep this from touching them."

He didn't bother to ask who Swish was, assuming he might meet the person later, if they survived. "Let's hope." He tried not to let pessimism undermine his confidence, fearing it might seep over to the others as well. He looked at Ryder with a cocked brow. "And your Daisy was content to remain behind?"

"Only because of the baby," said Ryder. "She's made a lot of progress in learning how to defend herself and fight, and I have no doubt she would've nagged me to come along if she hadn't been protecting our child."

"Congratulations," said Quinn, though his voice locked any warmth or sincerity. The idea of his brother facing the situation of an Omega expecting his child sent a chill through him, and he couldn't find it in himself to be genuinely happy for Ryder.

After some discussion, they planned their route into the house using thermal scanners from

Remy's ship that revealed the locations of all the beings on the planet. It updated in real-time, allowing them to plan the best route to avoid interacting with anyone.

They had one close call on the way to the house, but they ducked behind a stack of boxes waiting to be unloaded until the being had passed. After that, they were able to slip into the house, once again using one of Remy's toys to bypass the security system.

When Quinn eyed it with surprise. Remy seemed almost embarrassed when he said, "We had a good haul at the Antares Belt, and then just a few months ago, we found another ships' graveyard and salvaged what we could. There's a bunch still waiting, since it's practically undiscovered. The asteroid belt was part of an alien trade route long ago, before a safer route was found. It's pretty much been forgotten by the Coalition and humans."

"Nice," said Quinn, though his mind was focused on getting to Azaria rather than the wealth of his brother's friend.

Once they were inside, he could sense Azaria and smell her pheromones, though she smelled different to him. His brow wrinkled as he tried to identify it, and he followed his instincts toward her.

"There's a guard—"

Before Ryder could finish warning him, Quinn had already gone around the corner and punched out the Alpha coming to meet him. Nothing was going to stand between him and Azaria, and he didn't even need the tracking system Remy had provided him to find his way to her.

He burst into the room seconds later, a quick glance revealing what must be happening. There was an empty syringe on the floor, along with a half-filled vial of some injectable he was willing to bet was an enhancer. Garros had clearly given it to Azaria, but it didn't seem to have the desired effect.

She was still fighting him every step of the way as he tried to drag her to the bed. Quinn let out a roar as pure rage flooded his veins, and he swooped in to pull Azaria from the mobster's arms. He pushed her away toward Ryder, who steadied her, not looking back as he focused on Garros. "My Omega," he said with another rough growl.

"I paid for her," said Garros, sounding incensed. "You're the one who stole her."

"She's not yours to buy." He

lunged forward, hitting Garros in the face and knocking him down. The Alpha beneath him was smaller, but he seemed inclined to cheat. When he tried to poke Quinn in the eyes, he brushed aside his hand like it was nothing and punched him in the face once more.

The man beneath him slumped and groaned, clearly on the edge of passing out. "Mine," said Quinn again. The word was more animalistic than human as he lifted a hand. "Come here, Azaria."

She rushed to his side, either because she wanted to, or because his tone compelled her. He didn't know or care which right now, though he didn't like the idea of controlling her as Garros had tried to do. He pulled her against him, not looking away from Garros's gaze for a moment. "My Omega."

He lowered his head then, pulling her into his arms and positioning her so he could find her neck easily. He nuzzled the scent gland there, and just smelling and licking it was enough to excite him to the point he could claim her. He didn't allow himself any doubts, or to question that he was doing the right thing.

He'd vowed never to do such a thing again, but now that the moment was at hand, he didn't allow any doubts to stop him. He bit her, making her whimper since she wasn't in a state of arousal at this time, but he tried to be quick about it. There would be time for pleasure later, when they were all safe.

He pulled away, wiping her blood off his lip as he stared down at Garros. The other Alpha's disgusted expression revealed how little interest he now had in Azaria, who would smell like Quinn. It would've been physically impossible for Aldrich to take her even if she'd offered herself willingly. He grinned savagely at the man. "You're a scourge on the system." Without another word, he pulled out his gun and shot Aldrich between the eyes.

Only Azaria gasped slightly, but she didn't seem too bothered by his actions when he stood up. Neither Remy nor Ryder showed any disapproval, and they likely shared his assessment that he was doing everyone in the quadrant a favor by getting rid of the scum before he had a chance to gain more than a foothold.

They used the navigation system from Remy's computer to evade other lifeforms as they made it back to their ships, and when they stood outside, Ryder said, "We should destroy their ability to get off the planet."

"We should raze it all," said Remy.

With the three of them having decided on a course of action, Quinn picked up Azaria, not allowing her the option of riding on a different ship as the gangplank to Remy's ship dropped open, and Daisy came running out. She went first to Ryder, embracing him, and then turned to Azaria, who was dangling over Quinn's shoulder. "You're safe?"

Azaria grunted. "I guess."

"She's safe, but her place is with me." He nodded at Daisy and Ryder before doing the same to

Remy. After that, he returned to his ship, still carrying his Omega, and he placed her carefully in the copilot's seat moments later when they were in the command room again. "We have something to finish up here."

She nodded. "I heard, remember? I was there, after all."

He shrugged a shoulder. "I wasn't sure how traumatized you were."

"A lot less traumatized when I realized his enhancer wasn't going to work for whatever reason."

He barely glanced at her, having interpreted on his way back to the ship what her change in pheromones meant. "It's because you're pregnant. Enhancer doesn't work when you've already been bred."

She stiffened, licking her lips. She looked nervous as she slanted him a glance. "You know?"

"I have for the last few minutes." He shot her a grim look. "We have a lot to discuss, but I have to focus on finishing the mission first."

She subsided into silence, looking away from him, and he tried not to let his thoughts dwell on the new reality of his situation—he'd broken his vow to himself to never claim another Omega, and she was pregnant. His vasectomy must've failed, and he wondered if he'd been cheated by the doctor who did it several solar cycles ago, or if his body had simply healed itself afterward. He knew that had been a risk at the time, since many Alphas had accelerated healing ability, but he'd foolishly trusted in the procedure, never wishing to go through the pain of losing a child again.

"We're ready," said Remy."

"So are we," said Ryder.

"I'm ready as well." He pressed the firing mechanism after their ships aligned, sharing the common target, and focused all their firepower on destroying what they could of Garros's operation.

It wasn't just to remove him from the quadrant. They also didn't want to allow anyone remaining alive to have a way to follow them.

When they flew away from the planet moments later, it was a burning heap they could see from space, and he was satisfied they had ended the Garros Empire and any threat of retaliation.

CHAPTER FIVE

It was nearly an hour later before he spoke to her again. Azaria had spent the last sixty minutes in silent agony, wondering what he would do or think now that he knew. He'd claimed her in front of Aldrich, and in light of the fact he had destroyed the mobster, it seemed like overkill. She couldn't discern his motivations or why he was doing what he did in any respect.

He hadn't even given her a choice, though she supposed if

she'd said no, he would've let her go. At that moment, locked in his arms with him about to bite her, the last thought in her mind had been rejecting him. It had felt so right, and now she wondered how she'd deluded herself so thoroughly.

It was obvious he didn't want an Omega, and she didn't want him. She barely knew him, and what she knew of him wasn't appealing. So what if he had all the qualities that made a good Alpha? He also didn't seem to care about taking care of her, and he clearly didn't want anything to do with loving her. She and her baby would be better off at the convent.

"I'd like a ride back to Paladin please."

He froze for a moment before looking at her. He grunted. "No."

Her mouth dropped open, and she scowled at him. "What do you mean, no? You don't get to tell me no. I want to go home."

"You are home. Adjust."

She was perilously close to screaming at him in rage, and she did her best to pull it back with several deep breaths. "I think it's obvious you acted in a rash moment back there. You didn't want to claim me, and I didn't want to be claimed. Just take me home, and that's the end of it."

He scowled as he looked at her,

turning his chair and finally focusing on her. It was a bit daunting to be pinned under the intensity of his expression. "Have you ever bonded with an Alpha before?"

She shook her head. "No, of course not."

"Do you understand the bond at all?"

She hesitated for a moment and then shrugged. "I dunno. Not really. I know it's something an Omega should try to avoid at all costs."

He snorted. "I can't exactly argue with you there. Unfortunately, once the bond is established, we're stuck with each other. It's a physical connection, but it goes deeper than that. Too long of a separation can cause either one of us to go mad. If I'm not continuously renewing my claim on you, you lose the protection of carrying my scent too. I won't allow you and the child to take that kind of risk."

She tipped her chin. "It's not yours, you know. After all, you had a vasectomy." She tried her best to sound confident and scathing at the same time.

His eyes narrowed, but he simply lifted one side of his lip, which could've been a curl of disdain or perhaps amusement. "Don't be ridiculous. We both know it's my child, though I should consider asking for my money back on that vasectomy."

She crossed her arms over her chest as she glared at him. "If you ever really had one. Maybe you just said you did so I'd be forced to carry your seed. Isn't that your biological imperative?"

Any sense of humor disappeared from his face. "The last thing I'd ever want is to impregnate you. It's been done, and now we have to deal with the consequences. It's my role to keep you and the child safe. We're stuck together, so adapt."

She leaned back with a huff, looking away from him. "When

you phrase it like that, how can a girl resist?"

The sound he made was ambiguous, and he looked away from her, returning his attention to the computer. "We're heading to my home planet."

She wanted to argue, but she realized it was just to be contrary because she was still angry. She didn't have a better destination in mind, since he refused to return to Paladin. "Where is it?"

"Less than a day via ionospace. We could speed up travel time with a boost gate, but I'm not inclined to pay the toll."

She shrugged. "I guess it doesn't matter how long it takes. What's it like?"

"There are a couple of larger cities, but I live in one of the smaller outlying ones. There's not much to do there, but I don't spend a lot of time there. The rent's cheap, and it gives me an address to register my ship with the Coalition. It has a comfortable enough house, so you won't be living in squalor or misery."

Something about the way he phrased that raised her hackles. "I? Where will you be?"

"I'll be there too. I live there. I have a salvage operation to finish up though."

"I'll go with you."

He shook his head. "No, you

won't. I want you somewhere safe."

She glared at him. "What happened to that drivel about not being separated for long?"

"A couple of weeks isn't going to cause either one of us to go mad. I was talking months and years."

She prodded at him for the next hour, trying to get more information or convince him to allow her to travel with him, though she wasn't certain why she wanted to. The idea of being stuck in the small ship with him for weeks on end didn't sound appealing in his current state. He was a bastard, and she mourned that she was tied to him. Even if he hadn't claimed her with his bite, the child still would've been a link, though she hadn't ever fully committed to the idea of telling him.

"I'm glad you called me." They were the first words he had spoken to her in more than an hour.

She jumped, startled. "What?"

"When you got in trouble… I'm glad you called. It's my duty to take care of you, and it will be easier for both of us that you recognize it."

She glared. "It won't be easier, because I don't recognize that. I can take care of myself. Normally, anyway. Being kidnapped by a bunch of Alphas was a different prospect, and that's the only reason I called you."

His lips twitched as he looked at her for a moment. "And you just happened to have my frequency in your contact list?"

Her mouth dropped open, and she closed it quickly as she glared at him. "I looked it up because I thought maybe I should tell you about the baby at some point." She looked away from him, heat flooding her face as she refused to admit there'd been even a hint of anything more to it.

"I hope you would have gotten around to telling me eventually," he said with a hint of bitterness.

She looked at him again. "Don't try to be angry with me. You don't deserve a say in anything. You fucked me and cut me loose, and that was it. You didn't want to be my Alpha, and I didn't want to be your Omega. I thought I couldn't get pregnant based on what you said. This child is mine, not yours."

He looked at her for a long moment, his expression impossible to read. "It's mine whether you like it or not, and I'm going to look after both of you. You might as well accept that."

"Sure, after you dump us for who knows how long." She

looked away again, too angry to continue the conversation.

Maybe he felt the same way, because he subsided into silence, and they barely spoke for the rest of the journey.

CHAPTER SIX

He completed what should have been a four-week job in two-and-a-half, working long hours and cramming the hold full of anything valuable from the wreckage sites. It was enough to properly look after an Omega and a child on the way and provide the finest medical care available. He would ask her input about moving from his planet for the time being, wanting to take her to one of the more centrally located Coalition planets with better health care available.

He'd spent the last seventeen days working to the verge of exhaustion, but it had done little to shut down his mind. When he'd first left her behind, his plan was to use the time to ensure he maintained distance between them. He wanted her to practically hate him and want nothing to do with him. It was the only way to keep him from loving her, since that bond was already likely to form anyway now that he'd claimed her. Proximity and time would only lead to caring more and more for her, and he couldn't imagine doing that again.

Somehow, it hadn't worked.

Despite his resolve, his thoughts had centered around her, not in how he could keep himself from falling for her. Instead, there'd been random snatches of memory that came to him, both from the brief time he'd claimed her, and from their interactions at their last meeting.

Every time he thought of her, he associated it with anger—her anger, not his. He would've preferred it if he could have been angry with her and resented her for being part of his life, but his own actions had allowed the opening, and it wasn't like Azaria had seized upon it gleefully. They were both in the situation they were in due to outside influences, and he'd come around to the idea it was better just to accept that and be the best Alpha to her that he could.

He wasn't expecting much of a greeting when he arrived home that afternoon after selling his salvage, but she didn't even look at him when he walked into the house. She had been at the kitchen counter, looking like she was making something.

The room was redolent with the scent of spices, and his nose twitched in appreciation. He started to say something about it, but she took one look at him, went pale, and stormed away. She left her task half-finished, and he considered chasing after her, but he accepted her anger was justified.

She probably truly hated him, and that had been his goal to start with, but now it felt wrong. They were going to be bound together for a long time, at least the rest of their lives until one of them died. After that, she might be able to free herself from the link between them, but he didn't want to contemplate that. He realized he didn't want this cold, unhappy union with her. He wanted her to see him when he arrived home and smile, or better yet, to have her working alongside him at the next operation.

He groaned and wiped a hand down his face as he realized just how badly he had screwed up everything. She represented another chance at happiness, a chance he'd denied himself and refused to ever contemplate in the past, and now he'd done his best to sabotage it, to ensure it could lead nowhere happy for either of them.

With a sigh of disgust at himself, he left the kitchen and went down the hall, deciding a real shower would feel good after being confined to the tiny space on the ship for the last seventeen days. Once clean, he wrapped a towel around his waist and walked into the bedroom, startling her in the process.

She glared at him, hands on her hips. "What are you doing?"

He arched a brow. "I'm getting some clothes. Unless you prefer me naked?" He asked that playfully as his fingers went to the knot on the towel.

"Don't," she said sharply, but the way her nostrils flared and pupils widened betrayed she wasn't entirely opposed to the idea, though she might want to be. "That's not funny."

"I'm not trying to be funny." He moved closer, drawn by the scent of her. She smelled different this time than she had last time, likely because she was in a different stage of pregnancy.

He could see the faint outline of her stomach protruding through the jumpsuit she wore, and he realized she was still wearing the clothes she'd worn before. He hadn't left her any credits, and she'd probably never needed a credit account living at the convent. He frowned at the oversight. "Have you had enough to eat?"

She seemed surprised by the note of concern, but she nodded. "You had enough food."

He walked forward, putting a hand on her shoulder. She

stiffened, but she didn't shrug it off. "I'm sorry, Azaria. I behaved badly. I never expected this to happen, and I just dropped you here with a need to escape, wanting to put distance between us. It didn't occur to me to think about your needs in any fashion, and that makes me a selfish Alpha."

She didn't argue. She simply nodded as she looked at him, her gaze revealing nothing. "What changed? You're back a lot earlier than I thought you'd be, judging from what little you said before you left."

He could see how she ached to be angry with him, and how she wanted to reveal no curiosity or softening at all to his presence, but he had a feeling it wasn't in Azaria to be cold and withdrawn like that. "I worked like a dog, eighteen-hour days to finish what should've taken a month in two-and-a-half weeks. I wanted to get back to you."

She scoffed when she looked away. "Sure, you did."

"I did." He put his hand on her chin, turning her face back to his. "I didn't want to be with you, but that's not because of anything you've done, Azaria. I have good reasons for avoiding this sort of situation, but there's no escaping it now. I missed you while I was gone, and despite my best efforts to try to keep any emotions from forming, it was too late. I think it might've been too late from the moment I first saw you trapped in that box, writhing with pain and need. You called to the Alpha in me then, and you still do now."

Her lips trembled, but that was the only sign of his words getting through to her. "How am I supposed to believe you? You've never acted like you cared about me at all."

He closed his eyes, his shoulder slumping forward. "I know. I've been a bastard, but I'm hoping you'll give me a second chance to prove I can be a good Alpha to you and our child."

"I just don't see that happening." She turned away from him then, seeming final in her decision. If her shoulders hadn't been just as slumped as his, and if she hadn't trembled slightly, he would've accepted that. But seeing evidence that contradicted her words, he reached out for her instead, pulling her back against him and wrapping his arms around her.

She moaned even as she tried to pull away when he pressed his mouth against her scent gland on the side of her neck, licking and nuzzling until she relaxed in his arms. If he couldn't get through to her any other way, he was certain they could communicate through passion. He just needed her to relent enough to see he was serious about making this work in a way that made them both happy.

She resisted for a moment longer before her arms came around him. Quinn groaned low in his throat, purring against her scent gland, which made her whimper in need. Her pheromones drenched him, and he could smell the slick she produced in her arousal. He lifted her into his arms and carried her to the bed, holding his breath as he laid her down, half-expecting her to refuse him. She was capable of clear thinking and resisting her biological imperative when she wasn't in estrus.

When she pulled open the fasteners on her jumpsuit, he dared hope she was responding to him for an entirely different reason than their basic biology. He wanted Azaria to want him as a man, not just an Alpha.

He dropped his towel before joining her. He wanted to take his time to explore her, but it had been too long since he'd had her. Having her in his arms was intoxicating, and his mouth devoured hers, though she wasn't shy about responding.

He tasted her repeatedly, his tongue dipping between her lips as his cock nestled against the heat of her core. He rubbed the head deliberately against her clit, making her gasp and produce more slick. He couldn't deny his need to taste her, and he wrenched his mouth from hers with monumental effort.

She seemed dazed, and he didn't give her time to compose herself or second-guess what they were doing. Instead, he slid down her body and parted her thighs, inhaling her addicting musk before bending his head to lick where it dribbled on her puffed lips. She thrashed against him, twisting her hips, and he focused his attention on the little nub.

She cried out with need before calling his name. "Quinn, I…"

He growled low in his throat, nearly undone by the sound of his name on her lips instead of the generic "Alpha" she'd used during their last mating. He'd never heard anything more exquisite, and he was determined to pleasure her to the point where she'd never regret any of this. He redoubled his efforts, working his tongue around her clit before sucking on it several times.

She shattered, screaming his name again, which made his cock flex. He couldn't hold back as he moved up her body, parting her thighs and making a space for himself between them. She clenched her legs around him seconds later, and he stared down at her beautiful face. It was still painted in ecstasy as she rode the aftermath of her release, and he aimed to keep that expression on her face as long as possible.

He slid inside her carefully, aware she wouldn't be as accommodating when not in estrus, but he wouldn't be as large when he wasn't in rut. They fit together as beautifully as they had before, and he bottomed out inside her as she licked her lips and tossed her head.

"More, Quinn." She grunted as she strained against him.

He increased the frantic pace of his hips as he reached between their bodies to strum her clit. She whimpered and clenched around him at the additional ministration, and the micro-contractions of her sheath soon had him close to the edge.

When she came with another cry and spasm of her channel, he couldn't hold back. Grunting her name in a sound that was barely coherent, he surged deeply inside her and spilled his pleasure, mingling it with hers while wishing they could make every aspect of their future together fit so cohesively as the passion between them.

CHAPTER SEVEN

When it was over, Azaria rolled away from him, feeling like she'd betrayed herself as anger filled her. It was directed toward both of them—at her for being so weak as to succumb, and for him for being hot-and-cold. Even now, after the passion and care he'd shown, she didn't think she could trust him or believe he planned to be there for her and the baby. She wanted to fight any feelings growing for him, and she almost wished he'd never returned.

That was despite having missed him in the days he'd been gone. She'd done her best to fortify herself against any reaction to him and his inevitable return, and it had been easy in the beginning, especially when she realized he'd left her no credits, and she had no credit account established with the Coalition.

There'd been no way to earn any legitimate credits, so it had been a fortunate thing he'd had the pantry stocked and his home filled with things she needed. She could have reached out to Daisy if she needed to, but she'd been too humiliated by the situation to admit how dire it was, or how easy it had been for her supposed Alpha to leave her behind without looking back.

As the days passed, it was harder and harder to maintain her furious anger. As it inexorably faded, since such a thing wasn't emotionally sustainable without turning her into a bitter harridan, she'd started to think of him again in a different way. She'd resisted that then, and she resisted it now as she rolled out of bed and sat up before getting to her feet.

"Where are you going?" His voice was soft and full of concern.

Concern that was far too late, she told herself as she reached for his robe hanging on the bed frame and tied it around her. It was too big, but it would have to do for the moment. She just wanted to escape the room and the temptation lying in the bed. She didn't want to waste time looking for her clothing or talking to him while she was in a naked state of vulnerability.

Without bothering to answer, she left the room and stood in the hallway for a moment, not sure where to go. When she heard him approaching, she darted toward the kitchen and returned to the batch of cinnamon rolls she'd been making when he returned home.

Now, she started to scrape

everything into a bowl, intent on throwing it away. He didn't deserve the cinnamon rolls from the recipe handed down through her family for generations. He didn't deserve anything except a swift kick in the—

"What are you doing? Is it too old to make now?" He sounded concerned as he watched her from the doorway.

She grunted at him, still not bothering to answer. If she could just avoid looking at him, maybe she could avert the seduction in his eyes and deny her own weakness in wanting to yield to him. She cursed being an Omega, whose natural trait was to submit, though she couldn't help thinking there was more to it than that.

Part of her, the part that wasn't just controlled by a biological imperative, wanted to turn to him and throw herself into his arms. She wanted to revel in the way he held her, to experience his loving touch again, but she told herself that was all a lie. It was an illusion, or if it weren't, he'd change his mind again. She couldn't trust him to be consistent or to be there for her, and she'd be a fool to allow herself to fall in love with him only to be let down in the future.

"I can help you make a new…whatever it is."

She glared at him. "I don't want your help. I don't want anything from you." With jerky movements, she finished clearing the counter and tossed the dough into the trash. When she moved to the sink to clean, he was right behind her, pressing the button for her so she didn't have to. She watched as the counter cleared itself, and the self-washing cycle did the rest. She resented that too, having wanted the physical satisfaction of scrubbing it herself as both an excuse to avoid him and a way to work out some of her aggression.

He put his hand on her shoulder, and she resisted the urge

to look at him. "I thought things had changed."

"Maybe on your end, but not for me."

He sounded shocked when he said, "You were so warm and willing in my arms."

She snorted. "That's simple biology."

He was trying to get her to look at him, but she refused as he tugged lightly on her shoulder. "You weren't in estrus, and I wasn't rutting. You can't use that as an excuse."

She glared at him for a second when he finally succeeded in turning her head. "I didn't say it was because of estrus. It's normal for a healthy man and a healthy woman to indulge in sexual attraction. I don't think it's safe though."

He immediately paled and took a step back. "You're injured? Have I harmed the baby?"

Seeing his concern, she said, "I don't know. But I think you could, so you need to keep your hands to yourself." It seemed like the logical way to get him to step back and stop trying to entice her into falling for him, but she hadn't expected his complexion to turn almost gray, and he swayed, nearly falling before he reached out to brace himself with a hand against the counter.

"I'll go find a doctor and be back as soon as possible." He wasn't even dressed.

"It's fine. I don't need a doctor. I'm fine." She tried to calm him, but he wouldn't be reassured. He rushed to the door, pausing long enough to shrug on a coat that barely covered him, but would hide his state of nakedness. He was in a frenzy, and there was nothing she could do to calm him. As he rushed away, she realized he was genuinely concerned for her and the health of the baby, and she squirmed with guilt.

She didn't think they had done anything to harm the pregnancy, and what had seemed like a tactic to get him to leave her alone now just seemed like cruelty. She wasn't certain why it had affected him so much, but the idea of their sex triggering a miscarriage clearly devastated him.

She paced and nibbled on her lip as she waited for his return, and he was true to his word. He was back in less than twenty minutes, dragging someone behind him. She inferred the older man was a physician both by the bag he carried and by the long-suffering look he wore.

He took one look at her and seemed shocked. "I thought she was in labor."

"I said she was losing the baby,"

he snapped at the doctor as he glared at him. "Fix it."

"I can't just fix a miscarriage, sir." The doctor squared his shoulders and glared up at him, and she admired that the Beta male wasn't visibly intimidated by her Alpha. Perhaps he'd gone up against Alpha fathers before.

"I don't think I'm miscarrying," she said softly. "I was just afraid that maybe I shouldn't do certain things." She blushed. "While pregnant, I mean."

With a huff at Quinn, he approached. "I might as well examine you while I'm here, though it's clearly not a life-and-death situation as implied." With a look of chastisement in Quinn's direction, he took her arm. "Show me your room, ma'am."

"It's Azaria Khalid," she said as she led him down the hall. When Quinn followed, trying to enter the room, she barely bit back a giggle as the doctor slammed the door in his face and locked it, making it clear he wasn't invited. "It's amazing how you stand up to him."

The doctor exhaled, and then he trembled slightly. "It's not easy, especially to an overprotective Alpha, but some of these Alphas will try to run roughshod over common sense and all medical knowledge when it comes to protecting their Omegas."

She nodded. "I'm sorry you got dragged into this. I really don't know if there's any reason to be concerned. I just mentioned it might not be a wise idea to have relations right now." As she said it, she hoped the doctor would get the hint and back her up.

Instead, he frowned. "It's probably not necessary to abstain. Have you had any bleeding or other signs of problems?"

She shook her head. "But it's the first time since I got pregnant. It's probably wise not to do this right now, right?"

He might be brave, but he was also oblivious. "No, you'll find no reason to desist from normal relations unless there's a problem. Lie back, and I'll take a quick look to make sure, but I don't see any reason why you have to suffer. Even up through the day of delivery, sex is usually safe."

With a grunt of impatience, she laid down on the bed and allowed him to examine her. Knowing she'd brought this on herself did little to ease her irritation that the doctor hadn't picked up on her wanting him to inform Quinn it could be dangerous to have sex.

She'd abandoned the idea anyway by the time the doctor had finished. It seemed heartless to put him in a place where he believed there would be a risk when he clearly cared more intensely about the baby than she'd expected. Maybe he was genuine in his desire to reform and try again, though she wasn't ready to risk that just yet.

The doctor left a few minutes later after speaking with her, and then following up the conversation with Quinn, who was standing right outside the door when the doctor opened it.

He came in just after the doctor left, standing nearby and looking like he wanted to reach for her, but he didn't. "The doctor said everything's fine?"

She nodded. "He indicated

there was no risk."

He exhaled slightly, but he still looked troubled. "If I had realized it would place you in any peril at all, I never would have—"

"You didn't." She hated to see the suffering in his expression, and she disliked how she had led him to this. "I don't know why I said that. I mean, I didn't know anything about the situation either way, so I was just expressing a concern. That doesn't mean there ever was a valid risk."

"I still should have controlled myself. I should've known better. If you want me to leave until you have the child, I can do that. I'll do anything to keep you and her safe."

"Her?"

He flushed. "I'm sorry. Maybe you didn't want to know, but the doctor told me."

"I already knew. Sister Kathleen told me." She looked down, holding her hands together. "I was just looking for an excuse to keep sex from happening again. I didn't expect it to become this situation." She found the courage to look up at his inhaled breath.

He looked devastated anew, and then his shoulders slumped. "I understand." He turned away then, starting to walk out of the room.

"Quinn?"

He froze, but he didn't look back. "What?"

"I'm sorry. I wasn't trying to hurt you. I was just desperate to find any excuse. Do you understand?"

His voice was cold. "I fully understand the situation now." Without another word, he left the room, and she heard the door to the house close a short time later. She wasn't certain exactly what he thought he understood, and she didn't know what she wanted him to think. It seemed like she'd been successful in driving him away, but was that what she really wanted?

She didn't know, and she hated

the indecision almost as much she hated her lack of power in the situation. If she were truly his treasured Omega, she wouldn't have these fears and concerns. She wouldn't be trying to actively drive him away if she was secure in how he felt about her, but she was afraid to succumb to how she felt and to give in to the emotions trying to grow inside her. If he left her again, he would break her heart if she let herself love him.

But was it already too late to stop that? She had no answer, though she spent the better part of the afternoon trying to find one.

He was careful to avoid her for

the next few days, but at least he hadn't taken off again. They interacted occasionally, and he was perfectly pleasant, but cold and distant with her. Azaria was acting in a similar way, telling herself this was for the best. They could maintain cool civility until the birth of the child. After that, she didn't know what would happen, but it seemed obvious they weren't going to be together in a loving, traditional Alpha/Omega relationship. She told herself that was what she wanted, and sometimes, she almost believed it.

That evening, realizing he hadn't eaten the plate of food

she'd left for him on the table, she decided to take it to him instead. As she thought back, he hadn't eaten much at all the last few days, and he seemed withdrawn, as though it was taking a lot out of him to keep this distance between them. She was seeing that in herself as well, and she wondered if there was still a chance for them to find common ground and build a strong foundation that would allow them to be happy together.

It was a fanciful thought, and she wasn't certain she had any faith in it, but she was contemplating the idea of trying when she entered his office without bothering to knock. It didn't occur to her, but he jumped up from behind his desk, slamming down something to the surface as he barked at her, "What are you doing?"

She took a step back, trembling under the anger in his voice. He was deliberately using his Alpha tone, and she had to straighten her spine to withstand it. "I was bringing you some dinner."

"I'm not hungry."

She marched forward, slamming the plate onto the desk. "I don't care. You still need to eat."

"I'll eat later." He crossed his arms over his chest, and though he seemed angry, when she looked closer, his eyes were gleaming with moisture. Instead of rage, he was on the verge of tears. She wanted to ask him about it, but before she could figure out a diplomatic way to do so that diffused the anger between them, he moved around the desk and strode from the room.

She ran after him. "Where are you going?"

"I need a drink." With those words, he slammed the door behind him, and she imagined he was going to visit the bar down the street. He'd spent some days there recently, though he never came home inebriated. She figured it was just a place to hide away from her, but tonight, he seemed different.

She thought about going after him, but she was too curious about what had been on his desk to do so. Instead, she returned to his office, leaving the door open so she could hear if he returned, and walked over to his seat. She sat in it and looked down at the desk, quickly identifying a picture frame there. It was face down, and when she lifted it, she was surprised to see the supposedly unbreakable material had cracked under the force of how hard he had slammed it down.

It wasn't enough to obscure the image, and she saw sparkling blue eyes and long red hair blowing in the wind as a woman held her very pregnant stomach against the backdrop of a planet with lilac sand and a fluorescent green ocean behind her.

She turned it over again, looking for any indication of who the woman might be, but there was no identification, and there were no notes when she called up the comments from the "Settings" icon in the frame. Of course, if he knew who the woman was, he wasn't likely to need to record that information. She was clearly important to him, and Azaria was positive she had to know who this was to have the answers she sought.

It seemed unlikely he was going to open to her, especially not right now when he was out drinking after their angry exchange, so she turned to his comm system instead. It was locked, so she had to retrieve her wrist comm out of the bedroom she shared with him instead, tediously searching for Ryder's frequency and relieved to find it wasn't obscured. If he'd chosen privacy settings, she wouldn't have been able to find it at all.

She initiated communication with him. His face appeared on the screen, and he smiled. "How's it going, Quinn?" His voice trailed off as he realized it wasn't Quinn.

"Oh, hello, Azaria."

"Hello."

"Would you like me to get Daisy for you?" His expression changed, becoming softer. "She's struggling mostly with sickness at night. If you give her a few minutes—"

"It's not Daisy I called to talk to." She moved her wrist comm to reposition it as she walked back into Quinn's office.

"What do you need?"

As he finished asking, she brought up her wrist comm to show him the picture. "Who is she?"

Ryder hesitated, looking uncertain as she brought the wrist

comm back to her so she could see him, since he'd seen the picture now. "I really need to know, Ryder. I think it's important, and it might be the only way Quinn and I can resolve our differences and find a way to be happy together."

He sighed heavily, and then he nodded. "I'm not going to tell you everything, because I still feel like it's Quinn's story to tell, but Catriona was his Omega."

She dropped into the chair, shocked at the revelation. "He had an Omega before me?" It seemed impossible, especially since he'd been so reluctant to accept her as his Omega until his hand had practically been forced by Garros kidnapping her again.

"He and Catriona were both young when they recognized the bond. I don't know that she was his ideal Omega, but he loved her, and she loved him. They were going to have a child, and it ended badly." His expression tightened, and he swallowed hard. "There was nothing to be done to save either one of them, though I think Quinn still believes he could have done more. Shortly after losing Catriona and Javik, he told me he'd never claim another Omega again."

"What about—"

He shook his head. "I can't tell

you anymore. The rest of it needs to come from him. I'm sorry you guys are having trouble, but I hope you can find a way to make it work. You need him, but he needs you just as much, and he needs new hope for the future. He needs your child, though I think he's scared shitless about the whole thing."

She managed a small smile. "Who isn't? Thank you, Ryder. Give Daisy my best." With those words, she signed off and leaned back in her chair, thoughts heavy.

Quinn was clearly capable of love. He'd experienced it before, going so far as to claim an Omega and have a child with her. She could appreciate how losing someone—two someones—so important to him could destroy him.

He was clearly still grieving, and she had a better appreciation for why he hadn't wanted to claim her as his Omega, and why he'd seemed dismayed to learn about the pregnancy. When he'd taken active steps to ensure he never fathered another child, no wonder he'd been shocked and slightly appalled.

Yet he had stepped up, claiming her, and since he'd been home, he'd seen to her needs despite the distance between them. She recalled how warm and loving he'd been the first day he came home after being gone for seventeen days. If she'd responded differently, would he have found the ability to keep being that Alpha? Or would he have reverted to his hot-and-cold routine, withdrawing again?

She had been acting to protect herself over the last few weeks, and it was obvious he'd been doing the same. The question was, could they find a way to move past their hurt and fear, or was their relationship deemed to be this distant, cold thing until any warm feelings on either side died?

That was an intolerable thought, but she wasn't certain

how to overcome the problems between them. She had to try, and the first step was to try to stop shoving him away. Maybe if she softened a little, he would as well, and they would find a way to meet in the middle.

It was a difficult thought to contemplate, and her pride stung at the thought of being the first to yield in this war between them, but if someone didn't make a move, it would become a lifelong battle. Since she'd much rather have a harmonious and loving relationship, she had to be brave enough to take the first step.

CHAPTER EIGHT

When Quinn returned the next morning, she didn't mention he'd been gone overnight. He expected the same cold, angry silence as usual. Instead, she said, "I'm going to make breakfast. Do you have any preference?"

He started to tell her he wasn't hungry, but his stomach cramped then, reminding him he was. He'd spent all night at the bar, but he hadn't been consuming alcohol. He'd used it as a refuge to escape his house, ordering drinks he never really touched. The idea of losing himself in alcohol had been briefly tempting, but he didn't deserve that kind of reprieve. After nearly causing a miscarriage by rushing Azaria off to bed, he deserved every bit of suffering headed his way.

"Eggs." They sounded easy, and since she'd taken over care of the hens, they were sure to be fresh eggs. He was often gone and hadn't really bothered with anything besides basic care for them, since he didn't rely on them as a food source. If they hadn't come with the house, he wouldn't have had them anyway.

"I can do that. How do you like

your eggs?" She sent him a smile. It was a small one, but it appeared real.

He frowned, confused. He'd expected her to either completely ignore him or to launch into a tirade about him storming off. He certainly hadn't expected a gentle tone and conciliatory gesture of making his eggs.

"It seems silly not to know how you like your eggs, since we're living together." She made the comment offhand, not addressing the fact he hadn't yet answered. "I like eggs all ways except boiled. Maybe soft-boiled, but I hate a hard yoke."

"Huh." It wasn't the most

eloquent answer, but he spoke the word as he sat down at the table, still feeling bewildered. "I like soft fried."

"Sure thing." Her voice broke for a moment, and she seemed like she might not know how to make those as she stared down at the eggs. After a second, she blinked and started moving industriously again.

He watched her work, unable to break the silence. She didn't seem inclined to speak either, but it wasn't the same kind of cold silence they'd maintained between them for most of the last couple of weeks. Instead, this felt neutral for certain, and perhaps even soothing.

She bustled over to the table a short time later, placing a plate of eggs in front of him. She had one for herself as well, and he noted she'd made scrambled. He realized it was a strange thing to be discovering about her after all this time. How could they ever hope to have a happy relationship when they knew nothing about each other?

He'd been fooling himself with the brief idea of the tantalizing possibility that they could. He was certain she'd rather be back on the convent planet and would be happier there. If he weren't a selfish bastard, he'd offer to take her and the child and deal with the consequences of madness. It was far more likely to be the Alpha who went crazy from being denied his Omega than it was for an Omega losing her Alpha—especially when the Omega had no feelings for him besides mild contempt.

He couldn't bring himself to make the offer though. Maybe it was the right thing to do, but he wanted to keep her and their daughter with him. He'd already been selfish for half his life, so what was another half? Still, he wrangled at the guilt that tried to sweep through him before shutting it down. He could make her happy. He just had to find a way to do that.

"How are the eggs?" She seemed nervous, but she couldn't be that anxious about the state of his eggs and enjoyment thereof.

"They're good."

She took a deep breath, seeming to be drawing on her courage. He braced himself for a request, expecting her to ask him to take her back to Paladin. He was prepared to tell her no, but he realized he'd probably end up saying yes. If it would genuinely make her happy, it was his role to do that. It didn't matter how unhappy he was at losing her. He owed it to her to see to her needs, and if those needs didn't include him, he had to accept that.

"Did Catriona make your eggs like that?"

He stiffened at the sound of his wife's name on her lips. "What?" Iciness filled him, and he could see the regret forming in her expression. "What do you know about Catriona?"

She looked away from him, blinking rapidly. "I saw her picture in your office last night, so I called Ryder. He told me a little bit about the situation."

He stiffened further and pushed away his plate. "Betrayed by my own brother."

She looked at him, her

expression stern. "He wasn't betraying you. I explained to him that I thought maybe the information was the key for us finding a way to be happy together, and he agreed. He just told me the barebones, but he didn't tell me how you felt, or how you've coped since then. I need you to open up to me if we're going to have any chance to make this work, Quinn."

His first impulse was to push away from the table and leave the house again, but as he looked at her, her expression pleading for information, he couldn't deny her request to meet her halfway. "She was my wife. It wasn't just an

Alpha/Omega bond between us. I loved her, and she loved me, and we got married within months of bonding."

"Were you happy?" she asked after he drifted into silence again.

He nodded. "Happiest I'd ever been. When we found out we were having a child, I was happier still." He trailed off, slumping forward. He braced his head in his hand, blinking back hot tears that always plagued him whenever he thought of how happy he'd been.

"It was an easy pregnancy, and there didn't seem to be anything wrong. We weren't on a planet with a medical center, but there was a midwife and a few doctors, and it seemed sufficient for our needs."

He bunched his hands into fists as he recalled those last few moments, when Catriona had gone from smiling through her contractions to a look of fear crossing her face. It hadn't been pain but outright terror. She'd known something was wrong, and that was how he'd known too. "She hemorrhaged, and there was nothing they could do to save her or Javik."

The words were simple, but they didn't begin to describe how horrifying it had been to watch his wife and child die in front of him, her blood spreading in a large pool. He'd known she could never survive losing that much, though he'd clung to the desperate hope the doctor and midwife in attendance could save her.

"I'm sorry." She took his hand, her touch gentle. "That must have been devastating."

He found the strength to look up and meet her gaze as he nodded. "Nothing's ever been the same since. After burying her and Javik, I left the planet where we'd been so happy, and I made the decision I'd never take another Omega again. I didn't want to."

She licked her lips, her anxiety obvious. "Do you still feel that way?"

He groaned as he closed his eyes. "I have for years. I did until recently. I still want to feel that way, but I can't any longer. It seems heartless to turn away from you when I'm your Alpha, and I'm supposed to be taking care of you and seeing to your happiness."

She swallowed. "You deserve to be happy too. If my presence makes you unhappy, that's unfair to you."

He closed his eyes again, taking several deep breaths as he tried to restore his calm. When he opened his eyes, he could see sorrow filling her eyes. "You don't make me unhappy. I'm just afraid for you and for her."

She nodded. "I understand that, and I guess you've been trying to protect your heart and not love me? I've been doing the same thing, because I didn't think I could trust you. I thought you were just a selfish, inconsistent Alpha. I didn't realize there were good reasons behind your behavior."

He groaned. "No reason has been good enough to justify how I pushed you away. I left you on this planet without any way to take care of yourself."

She nodded. "You did, but you were also going to earn money to take care of us."

He frowned. "Don't make excuses for what I've done."

She shrugged a shoulder. "I'm not. I'm simply being pragmatic. Neither us have behaved in the best interests of forming a happy union. We've both been trying to protect ourselves from each other, and from keeping any emotion from developing. It's unlikely we could be happy that way, don't you agree?"

He sighed as he nodded, realizing she was about to ask him to return her to Paladin. "I'll take you home to the convent if that's what you want."

She gasped, and he looked at her again, seeing her shock. It quickly became anger that faded to hurt. "I see. If that's what you prefer, I'll pack." She started to stand up.

He let her, waiting until she'd walked near him before grabbing hold of her and pulling her into his arms, settling her on his lap. "It's definitely not what I want, but I thought it was what you wanted. I thought you were setting all this up to ask me to take you back to the convent after showing there's no future for us. The last thing I want is for you to walk away. I should be noble and let you, and I'm trying to be if that's what you need, but don't mistake that for me wanting it."

She looked up at him, her eyes earnest as she gazed at his expression for a long moment. Slowly, hope seemed to form in her eyes, and she licked her lips. "You don't want me to leave?"

He put his hand over her stomach. "I don't want either one of you to leave. I want you to be part of my life, and I think it's too much to ask for second chance, but I'm asking anyway. Do you think there's a possibility we could build something between us, something that will make us happy?"

Her lips trembled for a moment, and she blinked rapidly. "I think that's possible. As long as we're both working for it, and we let down our guards, I think it can happen."

"Does that mean you'll stay?" He held his breath as he waited for her answer, sensing everything important in his life hinged upon what she said next.

"Yeah, I will."

He embraced her tighter, holding her against him as he relished the feel of her arms embracing him just as firmly. They still had a lot of work ahead of them, but for the first time since he'd met her, he was hopeful he could have love and laughter in his life again, in the form of the delicate Omega in his arms and the baby forming in her stomach. It was strange to feel any sort of optimism for the future, and it caused a giddy sensation to sweep through him. His chest bubbled, and a rusty laugh escaped him. He hadn't laughed like that in years, but it felt good.

EPILOGUE

Quinn paced in the corner of the room, keeping a close eye on the situation as the doctors tended to Azaria, who was in the final stages of labor. The nurse had banished him temporarily to that spot so they could have plenty of room in case they needed to access any of the equipment he'd insisted they keep on hand.

He knew they were mostly placating him, and the doctor had reassured him repeatedly there was little risk of Azaria having any complications, especially on the same level as Catriona, but he'd still accommodated Quinn's demands.

Money likely had something to do with that, and he was thankful all over again that Remy and Maya had shared the location of their treasure trove of wreckage. With Azaria working alongside him—and it had taken a lot of persuasion on her part to get him to allow her to accompany him on the skid to retrieve materials— they had earned enough in weeks not to have to worry about their future for the next few years. Daisy and Ryder had been working alongside them, but they had departed first, deciding they had enough.

Quinn had been driven to retrieve at least two more cargo holds' worth in the intervening weeks, wanting to ensure he had enough money to pay for any complications that might arise. If nothing happened, which he hoped for fervently, then he would be set to provide a good future for his Omega and their child.

Perhaps she would even agree to marry him now. He suspected she had refused his proposal the last time he made it because she didn't want to be forced into marriage before their baby arrived. Perhaps she thought he would change his mind once Olivia was born, and she didn't want him to do that or feel like he was forced into it. Instead of badgering her to accept, he'd tried to take her rejection with good grace and redoubled his efforts to prove he loved her and wanted a future with her.

A welcome sound filled the room then, and his insides melted at the newborn scream reaching his ears. He rushed forward, crowding in so he could see his daughter as a doctor lifted her aloft, placing her on Azaria's stomach.

He moved forward, unable to resist the lure of his child's full head of dark hair. She had Azaria's darker complexion, but pale brown hair and more his shade of eye color. Olivia looked similar to the picture he'd received from Ryder three days ago showing his newborn niece, though she had Daisy's curly hair, and lots of it. Olivia wasn't bald by any means, but Corinne certainly had a lot more hair.

"Everything's just perfect," said the doctor before Quinn could ask. "Both your wife and daughter are healthy."

"She's not my wife… Yet." He turned to look at Azaria, who'd never been more beautiful despite the strain on her face, the perspiration dotting her brow, and the hint of exhaustion in her eyes. He smiled down at her. "Will you marry me now?"

She must've been tired, but she still managed a laugh. "Right this minute?"

"I'm willing to wait a few days."

She gave him a soft smile. "If you're sure that's what you want, then yes."

"It's what I want more than anything. I love you, Azaria."

She reached up a hand to him, and he quickly took it, not moving his other hand from Olivia's forehead as he basked in touching his wife-to-be and child. "I love you too, Quinn."

He closed his eyes, savoring how contented he was in the moment as a swell of pleasure filled him. She'd agreed to be his wife, though he'd considered her far more than that for months now. He was sure she was finally certain of him, as certain as he'd been of her from almost the day they'd decided to start again.

He had no hesitation about the future, and he was glad she'd yielded. He would make sure she had no regrets about loving him, planning to devote the rest of his life to making sure she was happy and loved, and would never think he regretted claiming his Omega.

ABOUT JUNO

Juno Wells grew up on Florida's Space Coast, watching the shuttles take off from Cape Canaveral. When she hit college, her childhood fantasies about space travel turned highly romantic. Now her mind reels with space adventures of fantastic alien lords in distant galaxies, and the Earth women they love.

Wells' stories explore the complex, sensual relationships between inhabitants of different star systems. There are always happy endings just as there is always a new world to explore.